FOS
7/98

# THE LION'S WHISKERS

## An Ethiopian Folktale

By Nancy Raines Day

**Illustrated by ANN GRIFALCONI**

SCHOLASTIC PRESS / NEW YORK

*To Meghan, Jesse, and Shelly, for listening, and to Ken, for believing.*
*My appreciation goes to Getahun Mintesnot for seeing that this retelling captures the flavor of his native Ethiopia.—N.R.D.*
*The illustrator makes grateful acknowledgment to Carol Beckwith and Angela Fisher for permission*
*to make collage-use of photo detail from African Ark (p. 39), published by Harry Abrams, Inc., 1990.*
*Photograph copyright © by Carol Beckwith and Angela Fisher.*

The story of a woman and a lion has been told around fires in Ethiopia for hundreds of years. This tale is most closely associated with the predominantly Christian Amhara people, traditionally the country's rulers. The Amharas are one of the few African tribes to write their folktales down.

Here's how to pronounce the names in this story:

Fanaye (FAH-nah-yay), Tesfa (TES-fa), Abebe (ah-BEB-beh).

Text copyright © 1995 by Nancy Raines Day
Illustrations copyright © 1995 by Ann Grifalconi
All rights reserved. Published by Scholastic Inc., *publishers since 1920.*
SCHOLASTIC and SCHOLASTIC PRESS and associated logos are trademarks and/or
registered trademarks of Scholastic Inc.
No part of this publication may be reproduced in whole or in part, or stored in a retrieval system, or
transmitted in any form, or by any means, electronic, mechanical, photocopying, recording, or otherwise,
without written permission of the publisher. For information regarding permission,
write to Scholastic Inc., Attention: Permissions Department, 555 Broadway, New York, NY 10012.
Library of Congress Cataloging-in-Publication Data
Day, Nancy Raines.
The lion's whiskers / by Nancy Raines Day; illustrated by Ann Grifalconi.
p.    cm.
Summary: In this tale from the Amhara people of Ethiopia,
a patient woman uses her experience with a wild lion to win the love of her new stepson.
ISBN 0-590-45803-5
[1. Amhara (African people)—Folklore. 2. Folklore—Ethiopia. 3. Stepmothers—Folklore.]
I. Grifalconi, Ann, ill.   II. Title.
PZ8.1.D3215Li   1995
398.2´0963´07—dc20
[E]      94-14453
CIP
AC
12  11  10  9  8  7  6  5                7  8  9/9  0/0
Printed in the U.S.A.              37
First edition, April 1995
Book design by Marijka Kostiw
The collages in this book were created with a variety of textured papers and materials,
including whisks from a straw broom for the lion's whiskers.

**O**nce there was a woman named Fanaye, who lived high in Ethiopia's mountains. Her home was a rugged place, with few other people. Fanaye longed for a family of her own. But a husband had never come her way, and she had grown too old to have children.

*Who would want me as a wife now?* she thought.

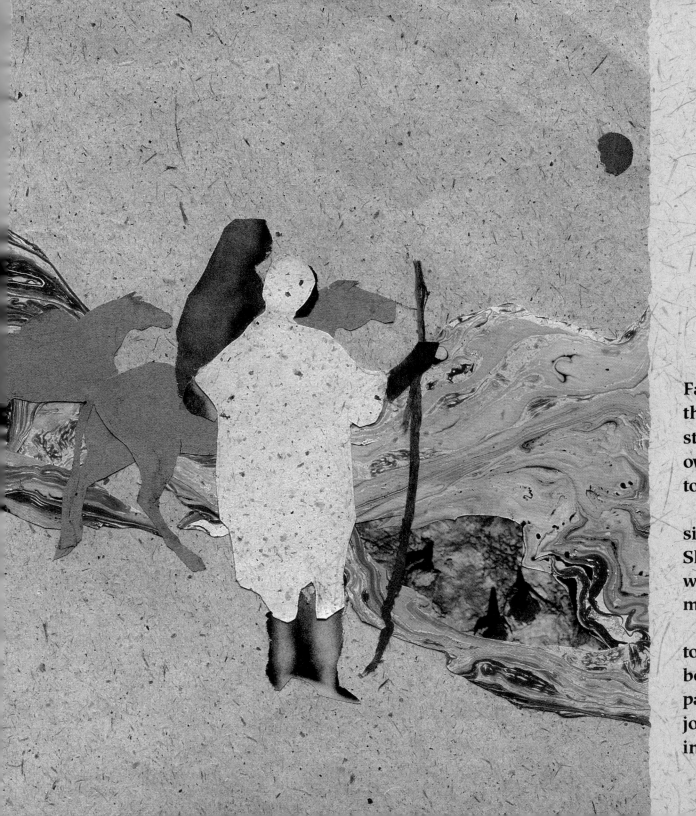

One day, when
Fanaye was fetching water at
the spring, a caravan of mules
stopped. A merchant named Tesfa
owned the caravan, and he talked
to Fanaye as his animals drank.

He spoke of his loneliness
since his wife had died of a fever.
She spoke of her loneliness
without a family in her tiny
mountain village.

Before long, the two agreed
to marry. Fanaye could scarcely
believe her good fortune. She
packed her few belongings and
journeyed with Tesfa to his home
in the flatlands.

I have a surprise for you," said Tesfa, ushering Fanaye into the fine stone house. "This is my son, Abebe."

"He is the child I have always wanted!" Fanaye cried. "Thank you, God, for sending me a son." She knelt to kiss the small boy.

But Abebe backed away. "Leave me alone," he said, scowling. "You're not my real mother."

"He is still sad that his mother is dead," Tesfa explained.

"I will love him all the same," Fanaye answered.

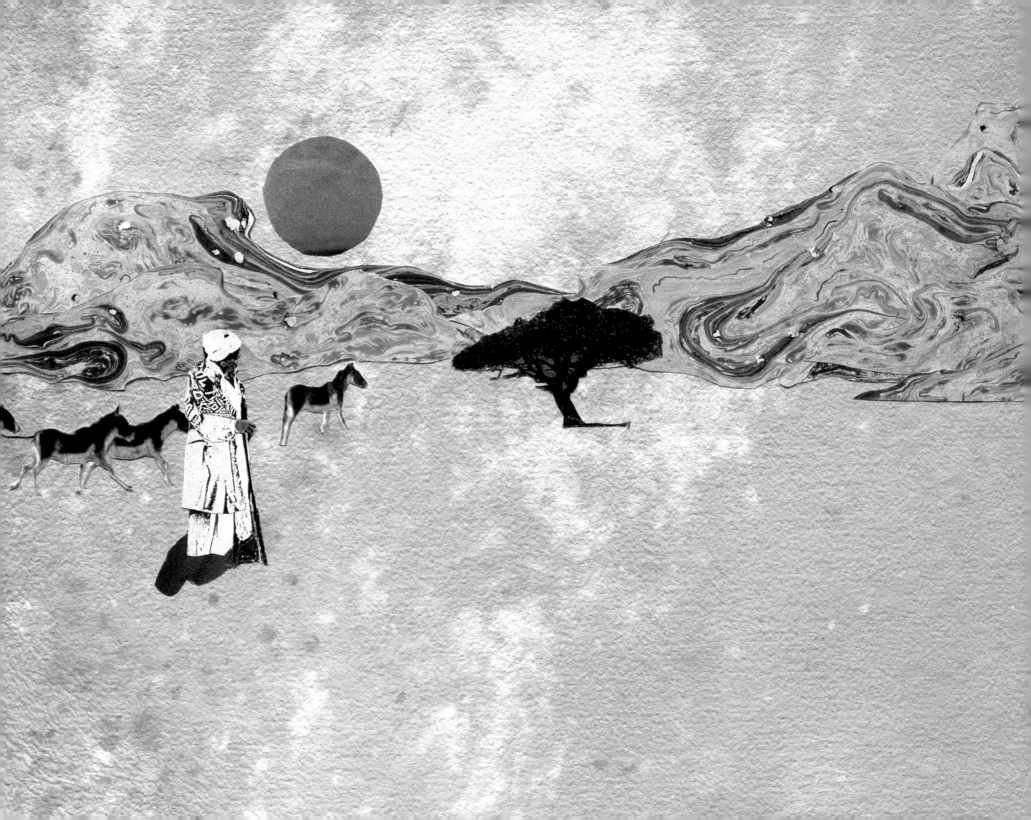

For days at a time, Tesfa would travel with the mules, buying and selling goods in far-off lands. He left Abebe home to tend their sheep, goats, and oxen. Fanaye stayed with Abebe, trying to be a true mother.

She cooked the thick, spicy stew called *wat* with goat's meat — her stepson's favorite. On her serving of the flat, spongy *injera*, she piled the tougher meat, saving the tenderest chunks for Abebe.

"I don't want any," Abebe said, pushing his portion away. "Your cooking isn't as good as my mother's."

And so it went. As soon as Fanaye mended his torn *shammas*, Abebe would run through the thorns and tear them again. As soon as she patched his handmade leather shoes, he would wade into the river and ruin them.

◈◈◈◈◈

"Come sit by me, and I'll read you a story," Fanaye offered one morning. Abebe, who loved stories, sat down. But when she put her arm around him, he jumped up.

"Don't try to act like my mother!" he shouted, and he ran into the forest.

Fanaye searched and called all day, but Abebe never answered. That evening, Tesfa returned, and only then did Abebe come out of hiding.

Fanaye cried all night long.

The next day, she set off for the cave of a medicine man known far and wide for his wisdom. Fanaye waited patiently among the many women who had come for cures and advice.

"Please," she begged him when her turn had come, "make a magic potion that will cause my stepson to love me as much as I love him."

"First," the wise man told her, "you must bring me the ingredients I require."

"Anything!" Fanaye promised.

"I need three whiskers from the chin of the fierce, old lion — the one that drinks from the river and prowls in the black-rock desert beyond."

Fanaye gasped. "But the lion will kill me!"

"Perhaps you can find a way," the wise man replied.

Fanaye longed to ease the ache in her heart. "I will," she vowed.

The woman spent a long night tossing, turning, and worrying. In the morning, she set off, telling no one of her quest.

Once across the river, she was scorched by the desert's dry heat. She trembled when she spotted the black-maned lion far in the distance. The ferocious beast picked up her scent on the wind and *ROARED!* Fanaye ran home so fast she could have won a race with a cheetah.

The next day, Fanaye took along some fresh meat. She saw the lion one hundred yards off. When she knew that he had seen her, she plunked the meat on a black rock and walked away. Over her shoulder, she saw the lion claim his meal.

The following day, Fanaye returned to the black rock. This time, the lion was fifty yards away. She laid out the meat, then ducked behind a boulder and waited. At last, the lion strolled up and gobbled the meat, casting wary glances in her direction.

Each day, the lion came closer and closer for his meat and watched Fanaye less and less suspiciously.

After several months, the day came when the lion walked right up to Fanaye. He looked into her eyes without blinking, then snatched the food right out of her hands. The lion's jaws opened so wide that she could count his long, pointed teeth. *Snap!* His jaws closed tight, ripping into the meat.

Fanaye stood her ground. Slowly she rubbed the lion's ear. Then she reached for his whiskers. *Pluck! Pluck! Pluck!* She had three hairs. The lion scarcely noticed. He licked his lips and strode off into the desert.

**F**anaye hurried to the wise man's cave. "Here are the three lion's whiskers you asked for," she said with pride. "Now Abebe will truly be my son."

The wise man flung the hairs into the fire.

"What have you done?" Fanaye cried. "All my work is for nothing now! Nothing!"

But the wise man smiled and shook his head. "You need no magic charms," he told her. "You have learned what you need to know. Approach your stepson as you did the lion, and you will win his love."

Fanaye sighed as she turned toward home. *Treat Abebe like the lion*, she puzzled. *What can that mean?*

A moment later, a smile spread across Fanaye's face, and her steps quickened.

Tesfa left on a journey the following morning. That evening, Fanaye heaped *wat* onto her own *injera*. She took a bite, smacking her lips. Abebe stole glances at Fanaye when he thought she wasn't looking.

After she had eaten, Fanaye set out Abebe's meal. In good time, she left the house. Only then did Abebe come to eat, but his food had grown cold.

The next night, Fanaye again ate first. After serving Abebe, she busied herself sweeping.

Abebe tiptoed over and sat down. He watched Fanaye's back warily while he ate the hot stew in silence.

**D**ay by day, as he saw that Fanaye made no move toward him, Abebe inched toward her. When she said nothing to him, he began to speak to her. At first, he talked only about the food and the weather.

As the weeks passed, Abebe began spinning stories about his flock and the village boys he played with. He liked the way Fanaye listened closely. His eyes shone as he talked, and he laughed more and more often.

**A**ll this time, Fanaye had pretended not to notice Abebe's torn *shammas* and ruined shoes. But *Timket*, the biggest holiday of the year, was approaching, and Abebe realized that he had nothing new to wear to the celebration of the baptism of Jesus.

"Fanaye," he asked politely, "could you please make me some new clothes? I promise I'll keep them nice."

Fanaye nodded. She wove and embroidered a fine white *shamma* and fashioned leather into sandals for Abebe. Fanaye hummed to herself as she worked.

**O**n the eve of *Timket*, Abebe linked hands with Tesfa and Fanaye as they joined the procession to the water.

❖❖❖❖❖❖❖

As the villagers' music, chanting, and dancing swirled around him, Abebe glowed. Tomorrow, he would feast with his family.

**S**oon after *Timket*, Tesfa's travels again took him away from home. One night, Abebe felt lonely at bedtime.

"Fanaye!" he called. "Will you read me a story?"

"Of course," she replied, beaming. "This one's about the time I befriended a wild lion."

"A wild lion!" Abebe's eyes grew wide. He snuggled close to Fanaye, not wanting to miss a single word.